For my husband and friend, Greg – whose father's heart inspired this story.

Love always, Christine Anne

x

For Ben

A.R.

First edition for the United States and Canada published in 2004 by Barron's Educational Series, Inc.

First published in Great Britain in 2004 by Orchard Books
Text Copyright © Christine Morton-Shaw 2004
Illustrations copyright © Arthur Robins 2004

All inquiries should be addressed to:
Barron's Educational Series, Inc.
250 Wireless Boulevard
Hauppauge, New York 11788
http://www.barronseduc.com

International Standard Book No. 0-7641-5802-3
Library of Congress Catalog Card No. 2004102086

Printed in Singapore
9 8 7 6 5 4 3 2 1

Itzy Bitzy House

Christine Morton-Shaw

Arthur Robins

BARRON'S

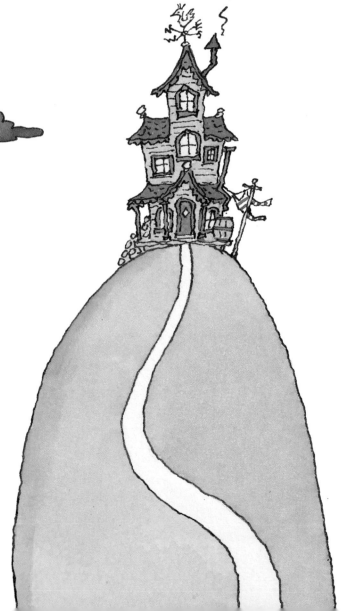

By an itzy bitzy house,
Down a twisty turny lane,

A twitchy witchy mouse
Is sitting in the rain.

From his snuffly wuffly nose
To his pitter patter feet,
He is drippy droppy droopy,
So he begins to squeak,

"Dry me! Dry me! Give me a home!
Nobody wants me; I'm all alone!"

But shh! What's that,

Sneaky peeky 'round the side?

It's a furry purry pussycat!

Quick, mouse . . . HIDE!

By an itzy bitzy house,
Down a twisty turny lane,
The furry purry pussycat
Is sitting in the rain.

From her splishy splashy whiskers
To her slinky dinky tail,
She is drippy droppy droopy,
So she begins to wail,

"Dry me! Dry me! Give me a home!
Nobody wants me; I'm all alone!"

But shh! What's that,

Sneaky peeky 'round the side?

It's a roly poly puppy dog!

By an itzy bitzy house,
Down a twisty turny lane,
The roly poly puppy dog
Is sitting in the rain.

From his shaggy scraggy coat
To his soulful doleful eye,
He is drippy droppy droopy,
So he begins to cry,

"Dry me! Dry me! Give me a home!
Nobody wants me; I'm all alone!"

But shh! What's that,
Sneaky peeky 'round the side?

It's a strutting butting billy goat!

Quick, dog . . . HIDE!

By an itzy bitzy house,
Down a twisty turny lane,
The strutting butting billy goat
Is standing in the rain.

From his curly whirly horns
To his prancy dancy feet,
He is drippy droppy droopy,
So he begins to bleat,

"Dry me! Dry me! Give me a home!
Nobody wants me; I'm all alone!"

But look! What's that,
In the rumble grumble sky?

IT'S
FLICKER FLASH

LiGHTNiNG!

Quick . . .
find somewhere dry!

By an itzy bitzy house,
In the middle of a storm,
The drippy droppy animals
Are trying to get warm.

But shh! What's that,
At the creaky cranky door?

A shimmer glimmer
gap appears . . .

. . . And then a bit more!

It is a wrinkly crinkly man
With twinkly winkly eyes,

He peeps under his umbrella
And takes them by surprise...

"I'll dry you, dry you! I'll give you a home!
It's me who wants you; you're not all alone.
I'll love you! Love you! My door's open wide
And we're all getting wet – so come inside!"

In the itzy bitzy house,
Down a twisty turny lane,
The cosy dozy animals
Look out at the rain.

'Round a crickly crackly fire,
Or on a wibbly wobbly knee,
This is what they sing
Every day at tea:

"We're snuggly cuddly in our itzy bitzy home,
We're warm and wanted; we're not all alone!